GRAY BOY

GRAY BOY

A STORY BY

JIM ARNOSKY

LOTHROP, LEE & SHEPARD BOOKS   NEW YORK

3 4 5 6 7 8 9 10

Library of Congress Cataloging in Publication Data
Arnosky, Jim. Gray Boy.
Summary: Despite his attachment to the young boy who raised him from
a puppy, Gray Boy gives in to his natural instincts and goes back to the wild.
1. Dogs—Juvenile fiction. [1. Dogs—Fiction] I. Title. PZ10.3.A86923Gr
1988   [Fic]   87-29337
ISBN 0-688-07345-X

This story is dedicated to Lucien Emerson,
author of over one hundred westerns,
who encouraged me to try
spinning a yarn of my own.

1

Gray Boy rolled over on his side and yawned his long red tongue into the afternoon heat. The lazy late summer day was too humid for a big dog to do anything but sleep. With one eye half-open, Gray Boy surveyed the world from where he lay on the Emersons' porch. He looked to the shed across the lawn, and beyond to the cornfields, hill farms, and the forested lump on the horizon that was Pine Mountain. Gray Boy's gaze lingered on that distant outline and, with the mountain in his mind, he drifted into sleep.

Gathering clouds stitched a dark quilt over the farm valley as Gray Boy snoozed. Then, with a flash of lightning and a rumble of thunder, rain poured. The soaking cooled the air and saturated the soil. Another crack of thunder awakened Gray Boy, and he sat up as the shower passed over the Emerson homestead and rumbled its way eastward to the village. When the sun peeked through the trailing clouds Gray Boy stood and shook off his lethargy, then romped down the porch steps into the yard and rolled vigorously in the cool, wet grass.

Gray Boy was about to give chase to a flock of chirping birds in the nearby cornfield, when an alluring smell stopped him. It was a mixture of dry reeds, the lingering odor of fish, and the

tang of ferns. The dog knew exactly what that
smell meant. He bounded back up the porch steps
to greet Ian Emerson coming out of the house.
Ian was carrying his fishing rod and the old creel
that had belonged to his father. Gray Boy sniffed
the creel closely and took in its seasoned scent.
He then ran happy circles around the boy as they
went together across the lawn toward the river.

The fishing hole wasn't far from the house,
but whenever Ian approached its banks he felt
like an explorer in a wilderness. At any moment
a Great Blue Heron might rise from its stand near
the stream bank and flap ghostlike over the
water. Or one of the river's big Brown Trout
would splash on the surface after a floating insect.

While Ian knelt in the cinnamon ferns and
stared down into the water, Gray Boy mean-
dered downstream to explore on his own. Ian

tied on his red-and-white spoon lure. The pool shone amber around its shallow perimeter and deepened to a mysterious, murky green in the middle. From his kneeling position in the tall ferns, Ian cast the line out into the center of the pool.

He hadn't even begun to work the lure before a large fish leaped high out of the water and splashed back down into the murky green. Startled, Ian wasn't aware that the big trout had taken the spoon lure and was on his line, until the reel's crank handle clobbered his knuckles as the fish dashed upstream in an effort to break free. Ian clambered to his feet and stood in the ferns. He needed to slow down the tugging fish. With his right hand he held tightly onto the rod handle and, with the fingers of his left hand, he fumbled to set the reel's drag knob. Instantly, the trout jerked the whole works from Ian's hands. Ian dived frantically into the ferns and grabbed the rod just as it was being pulled over the bank and into the stream. He wrapped both hands securely around the butt of the now straining rod and yanked backward with all his might.

This stopped the fish's upstream movement and gave Ian a chance to crank in some line. The huge trout began to run again, this time downstream toward its antagonist. When the fish was just ten feet away, it burst up out of the water, leaping wildly into air. Its brilliantly speckled side flashed in the sun. Ian couldn't believe his eyes. The Brown Trout had to be well over five pounds! Ian held his ground and called downstream to Gray Boy.

"Gray Boy! Come look at this monster!"

Gray Boy had been nosing around a

crayfish in the shallow water. When he heard Ian's call, he lifted his dripping muzzle from the cool stream and cocked an ear in the boy's direction.

"Gray Boy! Quick!" Ian shouted. The big dog climbed up the sandy bank and raced toward the sound of Ian's voice.

Ian's hands were getting tired. The big trout made yet another powerful run upstream, but Ian was too good a fisherman to lose his head so late in the battle, and the fish's effort to escape was thwarted once again.

By the time Gray Boy reached Ian, the trout was played out. Exhausted, it rolled over on its side in the water. Ian now only had to crank the heavy fish to shore. He reeled in line slowly, pulling the fish broadside through the pool. Ian's heart was thumping madly as the monster trout neared the river bank. Gray Boy was just as excited, and he barked loudly. The trout's dead weight suddenly broke the fishing line and Ian felt his rod go limp. Gray Boy stopped barking and he and Ian watched silently as the fish drifted away from the bank and sank sideways into the deep water of the pool. Ian threw his rod down in disgust and angrily kicked a mound of sod from the bank.

Gray Boy plunged into the stream and circled the spot where the trout had sunk. Then he dived out of sight. Ian had never seen his dog dive so deeply before. He watched in awe for what seemed like minutes, but were actually only seconds, until the dog emerged with the glistening fish clamped in his mouth.

"Gray Boy! You got him, you got him!" Ian exclaimed. Happy tears ran down his sunburned cheeks. "Bring him here, boy, over here!"

Gray Boy paddled to shore and hopped onto the bank. The big dog gave a great shake and shed water all around, with the fish still clenched firmly in his jaws. Ian reached to take it, but Gray Boy was reluctant to give up his trophy. He growled as though to say the fish was now his.

Ian instinctively sensed danger. Gray Boy had never before growled at him in just that way.

"Good boy," Ian said calmly. "Good boy."

Gray Boy hunkered down, the trout still clamped in his mouth. Another, deeper, growl rumbled from his throat. Ian persisted with gentle coaxing. Gradually, Gray Boy slipped out of his sullen mood. Finally, he relinquished the prize.

Ian pulled some cinnamon ferns from the bank and neatly lined the old creel. On this fragrant bed he laid the trout and then closed the creel, as best as it could be closed with the fish's speckled tail and spotted head sticking out on either side of the woven lid.

Gray Boy sniffed the stuffed creel, hopped happily into the summer air, and let out a loud "Woof!" He and Ian then turned from the stream and started home.

2

Autumn filtered into the farm valley. Here and there a brilliant red leaf stood out among the green ones. Early changing maples stained the scene like open cans of orange paint thrown smack against a summer canvas. Soon every changing tree had hoisted its flag of color: birch yellow, beech brown, oak red, sugarbush orange, and tamarack gold.

The crisp, cool air of the new season

brought about a change in Gray Boy. He became full of energy and was always on the move. He made regular rounds, investigating the smells of mice that had moved from the nearby fields to their winter quarters within the foundations of the Emersons' buildings. He followed the scents of chipmunks and squirrels that were busy gathering and storing food. Gray Boy ranged away from the house and yard to the edge of a nearby woodlot. There he flushed wild birds from the cover of tangled brush.

School had started for Ian, and his mother, Lucy Emerson, had returned to her job in the school cafeteria. Ian caught the school bus early each morning. Lucy had a couple of hours for housework before she had to leave for school. Gray Boy was alone until Lucy returned, an hour or so before the school bus brought Ian back.

This routine had worked well the last school year. During school hours Gray Boy had stayed on the Emerson property. The year before that he was only a pup and had been confined to a pen. This autumn, however, Gray Boy didn't follow last year's pattern and began wandering away from home. He frequently was nowhere in sight when Lucy left in the morning and was not always there to greet her in the afternoon.

One afternoon, Lucy found a large river rat lying dead on her doorstep. When Gray Boy loped up to greet her she noticed the dog's legs were covered with mud. Lucy knew he had been down at the river. It was he who had killed the rat and brought it home.

When Ian came home from school he thought it funny that Gray Boy had gone alone to the river and killed himself a rat. But Ian's mother saw it differently. It was becoming clear to her that Gray Boy was not entirely trustworthy.

A full-grown dog roaming free was a liability in a country of deer herds and dairy cattle. Things were hard enough for a young widow with a thirteen-year-old son, without having to cope with a lawsuit from an irate farmer. On the other hand, Gray Boy was generally a good dog. He was a mixed breed—part this, some that, with a lot of Newfoundland. Lucy knew Newfoundlands to be lovable giants who adore people and are fantastic swimmers. There are hundreds of stories of Newfs who have dived into dangerous waters and saved drowning victims.

The Newf in Gray Boy was physically apparent. His body was huge and barrel-chested. His paws were bear-sized and webbed between the toes. His head was massive, with short floppy ears, and his long red tongue usually hung down out of his mouth. Just looking at him made it difficult to stay angry with him, no matter what his transgression.

Gray Boy had been a gift to Ian from his father just weeks before he died in an auto crash. Though Lucy worried about the big dog, she rejected any thoughts of getting rid of him. She decided to forget about the incident with the rat.

But each morning, after walking with Ian to the school bus, Gray Boy found a longer way back home. He traversed cornfields and circled meadows, exploring different farms in the river valley. One of these farms belonged to Randolph Agosto.

Mr. Agosto raised a barnful of rabbits, which were neatly housed in various wire cages and runs. Each chicken-wire hutch had a watering tube and a small wooden tray to hold feed. The floors of the hutches were constructed of heavy, woven hardware fencing, which allowed the rabbits' round, pelleted manure to fall through and pile up on the earthen barn floor. The smell of the manure mounds escaped through the many cracks in Mr. Agosto's dilapidated barn walls. One windy day the scent was carried a good distance through the air. It reached the wandering Gray Boy and lured him over to investigate.

Mr. Agosto was hunched over in his garden, stripping the last dried-out soldier beanpods from their brown stalks, when Gray Boy appeared beside the barn. The dog crouched low, pressing against the faded clapboards to keep out of sight. When Mr. Agosto turned his back, Gray Boy slipped into the building as quietly as a coyote.

The smell of rabbit permeated every corner of the old barn. Ancient chords vibrated inside

Gray Boy, like music from an aboriginal instrument. The room became the hunting ground. The caged rabbits became the prey. Gray Boy singled out the largest wire hutch and crept toward it, every muscle in his body tense with anticipation. The rabbits in the hutch did not fear the dog. They simply went on with the business of eating and drinking. Inside their wire walls they felt secure.

One of the bigger does hopped over to the chicken wire and peered down at Gray Boy. She wriggled her nose and worked her jaws, munching on some piece of grain picked out of the tray. Her soft fur was a wolfish gray, and it rippled over layers of fat as she moved. Gray Boy fixed his eyes on her, watching every munch, every wriggle, until he could no longer stand the flood of rabbit that came over his senses.

3

Lucy Emerson wiped her hands dry and hung the dish towel on its hook near the slate kitchen sink. After working all day in the school kitchen, she'd had her fill of dishes and decided to let her own drip dry in their rubber rack. She picked up the daily paper and sat down to read.

Ian was busy on the porch cleaning up the mess a marauding skunk had made of the garbage bag. It was the third time in a week the skunk had raided the garbage can. An orange pickup pulled into the driveway. It was Bill Willum, Ian's uncle.

Lately, Bill Willum would often pull into the Emerson drive with Gray Boy in his truck, having found the dog wandering along the roadside. Gray Boy hadn't appeared for supper, so Ian figured his uncle must be bringing the dog home again. Ian ran to the truck and peeked into the open bed.

"Where's Gray Boy?" Ian asked.

"Darned if I know, boy," answered Uncle Bill. Then he added, "Don't worry about that dog, Ian. He can take care of himself." He draped an arm over Ian's shoulder and started up the porch steps. "I'll bet Gray Boy can handle anything an ornery wolf can!"

Lucy Emerson greeted her older brother with a kiss. She put a fresh pot of coffee on the stove and sat to visit. It turned out that Bill

Willum had come about dogs, but not about Ian's dog. He had just traded his old wooden canoe for a pair of fine hunting beagles, with which he hoped to hunt snowshoe rabbits in the Pine Mountain area.

"Gonna go pick them up in Warren after work on Friday," he said. "I think their names are Smokey and Hardtack." Ian perked up at the neat names.

Lucy poured her brother's cup full of coffee and said, "Well, I hope you can keep your dogs from roaming the way Gray Boy does." She glanced out the window into the twilight. "He's probably been gone all day . . . ," she worried. "It's near dark now and he's got me thinking all kinds of troublesome thoughts."

"He'll be back!" Ian spouted confidently.

Bill Willum changed the subject. "I was wondering if you had all those leather collars

Gray Boy grew out of. I could use a few if they're small enough."

Lucy turned to Ian, but before she could ask, he said, "They're out in the toolshed. I'll get them for you."

Bill Willum made use of the moments alone with his sister. His face became serious. "You know that dog is goin' to be trouble—more than you may think," he told her. "I didn't want to say this in front of Ian, but Gray Boy's growin' wild and he's too big for most folks to handle."

"I know, Bill," Lucy said, staring into her coffee cup. "He's even too strong for a heavy chain. But Ian loves that dog so. You and I and Gray Boy have been all the family Ian has had since Ed died. Ian and Gray Boy get along so well and, with us living away from the village and other kids, we need a dog."

"Lucy, the last time I picked up Gray Boy from the road, he snapped at me."

Lucy looked at her brother in alarm.

Bill went on. "And old man Agosto says he saw Gray Boy chasing a neighbor's foal. Says the dog was runnin' alongside that foal and nipping at its hooves and legs just like a wolf!"

Lucy shuddered. "If Gray Boy ever hurt somebody or something, it would just be awful. But what can I do?"

Bill poured himself more coffee. "I suppose to begin with you could sit down with Ian and talk it over with him. You and I both have been keeping our worries about Gray Boy too much to ourselves. If anything terrible did happen, it would be easier on Ian if . . ."

At that moment, Ian came through the back door, shouting as he ran. "Mom! Uncle Bill! Gray Boy's out back. He came home with something on his face. Come help me with him." But before the three of them could budge, they heard pounding on the front door.

"Who could that be?" Lucy exclaimed.

Ian and Uncle Bill went out back to Gray Boy while Lucy Emerson answered the front door. "Just one minute!" she scolded the pounding visitor. She flicked on the porch light, opened the door, and reeled back in horror at the sight of Randolph Agosto. Blood was smeared on his overalls and in each hand he held the mangled carcass of a rabbit. He stood in the dim light steaming with rage, not speaking a word, blood from the dead rabbits splattering on the porch deck. Lucy Emerson finally spoke.

"Randolph! Whatever has happened?"

"You know what's happened, Lucy Emerson!" Mr. Agosto exploded. "These were my two best does. That WOLF of yours broke into my

cages and tore half a dozen of 'em up! I came in
and caught him. He was covered with rabbit fur
and blood. Wire was strewn everywhere! He just
ripped through that chicken wire like it was
nothin'!"

Lucy was about to offer a distressed apology when Bill Willum came back into the house.
"Holy smokes!" he said loudly. "What have we
got here?" He motioned his sister to sit down,
then said calmly, "What is it that we can do to
cover your losses, Randolph?"

Randolph Agosto flung the dead bodies out
onto the dark yard and stepped inside the house,
shaking a bloody finger.

"Those were PRIZE DOES!" he shouted.
"That devil of a dog is goin' with me and the
constable first thing tomorrow morning. I called
Harry as soon as I could after I found that mur-
derer in my barn! If Harry wasn't busy tonight,

I'd have him here right now with a permit to
SHOOT that varmint!"

"Now hold it right there!" Lucy Emerson
warned Mr. Agosto. "If you want to come here
with the constable, well come. But don't throw
any more threats around my house!"

She was angry and Mr. Agosto backed out
onto the porch deck. Then, lowering his voice
and his manner, he repeated, "Tomorrow mor-
nin' . . . Me and the constable will be here to haul
that wolf-dog away. I don't know what Harry
does with killer dogs, but if I have my way, he'll
shoot that one dead!" With that, he stormed off
the porch and disappeared into the night.

Ian had heard it all from the next room.
Mr. Agosto's words rang in his head as he approached his mother and uncle. He held back
tears and said in a monotone, "It's chicken wire

. . . all stuck in Gray Boy's face . . . I can't pull it out, and it's hurting him." Tears came.

Uncle Bill took some antiseptic from his sister's medicine cabinet and went out to his truck to get a pair of pliers. Lucy Emerson walked close to her son. No words were spoken. A hug said it all.

4

Lucy and Ian held Gray Boy prone on the toolshed floor while Uncle Bill labored to remove the wire from the dog's face and mouth. After what seemed to all like an eternity, the job was done. Gray Boy was left alone inside the shed, to keep him confined until the constable came in the morning. The big dog was exhausted by the ordeal. His legs were weak and shaking. He plopped down on the wooden floorboards and slept.

"I'll be here first thing tomorrow," Uncle Bill said to Lucy as he crawled into the cab of his pickup. "Maybe together we can convince Harry not to take Gray Boy if you promise to keep him penned."

"Thanks, Bill," Lucy said. "I don't know what we would have done without you."

"Thanks, Uncle Bill," Ian said. Bill Willum drove out of the driveway and went home.

Later that night Gray Boy woke to find himself locked in the shed. His face was sore. He was confused. He paced back and forth in the dark room. After a while, he heard someone coming. The wooden door slid open slightly and Ian stepped inside. Gray Boy wagged his tail as the boy approached. Ian stooped beside his dog and stroked Gray Boy's thick coat.

"Now you've done it, boy!" Ian scolded

softly. "Old man Agosto is comin' in the morning with the constable. They're goin' to take you away unless Mom and Uncle Bill can talk them out of it."

Gray Boy sat back on his haunches and stared at the closed shed door. Ian looked into the big dog's eyes and tears filled his own. He sat on the shed floor and cried. He wished for another chance. As if he understood Ian's thoughts, Gray Boy licked a salty tear from Ian's cheek.

A crashing noise outside shattered the moment, and Ian jumped to his feet. "It's that skunk, I'll bet!" he said, wiping his eyes with his sleeve. "In the trash again. . . . I'm tired of cleaning up garbage!"

Ian reached for the small .22-caliber rifle that hung on the shed wall. Quietly, he loaded it with a cartridge, then walked over to the closed door. Gray Boy was alert, watching Ian's every move. Ian looked back at him and whispered a firm "Stay!" Then, with the .22 held upright and his finger on the trigger, he slowly pushed against the door. A crack of moonlight beamed across the floorboards as Ian peeked out toward the trash.

The skunk had pushed away the trash-can lid and was rummaging in the top of the garbage bag inside the metal container. It pulled with its claws at a tear in the thick bag and exposed more of the garbage inside. Ian pushed open the shed door and aimed the rifle at the broad *V* of white fur on the skunk's back.

The open door was too tempting for Gray Boy to resist. He ran through the opening, barreling Ian over in his escape. *Twang!* The rifle went off into the night sky and the scavenging skunk disappeared under the Emerson porch. Ian saw the direction Gray Boy had taken in the darkness. He sat on the ground and laughed at the thought of what a silly sight he must just have been. Then he picked himself up and answered his mother, who was calling from the house to see if everything was all right.

"Yeah, everything's okay," Ian said, still laughing. He brushed himself off and walked to the porch. "That skunk was in the trash again. I took a shot at it and missed. Gray Boy knocked me down and ran off." Ian stood beside his mother and looked out into the night. "Gray Boy ripped out of here so fast," he said, "I wouldn't be surprised if he makes it all the way to Pine Mountain. That's the direction he was headed in."

Lucy Emerson looked toward the mountain. She worried about Gray Boy getting into more trouble than he was already in. Then she said, "Oh well, I guess he won't do much harm in that wilderness." She looked at Ian. "No telling when he'll come back home this time." Then she patted her son on the shoulder and walked into the house.

Ian felt a secret joy in Gray Boy's escape. He hoped the dog would stay away long enough to send the constable and Mr. Agosto away empty-handed in the morning. He felt certain that Gray Boy would eventually come home and have another chance after all. Ian glanced once more in the direction of the moonlit hills, then went inside to join his mother.

5

Gray Boy slowed to a trot at the foot of a
hardwood ridge. He lifted his nose in the night
air and smelled the trees. He rolled onto his back
in glee. Nearby, a barred owl hooted and the big
dog ran to bark ridiculous circles around the base
of its tree. His loud yaps sounded out of place in
the somber woods. The owl swooped down off
its limb and Gray Boy felt a hush of wings as it
flapped over him and away into the shadows. He
shook his head, shedding the eerie presence of the

bird, then turned to run down a well-traveled game trail.

An old doe and her two summer fawns were walking along the trail when Gray Boy's scent alerted them. They froze in their tracks as the scent became stronger. The mother deer gave a snort and all three vanished up the ridge. Gray Boy had never smelled deer so close before, and his concentration deepened as he followed the leafy path. Since the deer tracks were fresh, he easily drew a bead on which way the animals had bolted. He coursed uphill, following the heady aroma.

The deer lived their lives along this ridge. The lay of the land was imprinted on their minds. When the trail sharply curved back downhill to a marshy hollow, all three raced down the curve in fluid motion.

In his excitement, Gray Boy overran the

twisting trail and lost track of which way the
deer had gone. He snuffled around the ground
until he had their scent again, and let out a
spirited yowl as he barreled downhill toward the
marsh.

The deer were standing at the edge of the
hollow looking back in Gray Boy's direction.
His clumsy crashes and thumps echoed in the
dark woods as he charged down toward them. As
soon as he appeared in the clearing, the old doe
snorted loudly and the three deer bounded away
in different directions. Only the doe lifted her
tail, flashing its white underside, and Gray Boy
plunged into the marshy muck following her
flag. The fawns were safe. They circled the hollow and returned to the hardwood ridge to wait
for their mother.

Gray Boy kept a close tail on the doe all
through the tiny swamp. His large, webbed paws

provided him with firm footing on the mushy ground.

The doe left the marsh and turned back along its brushy border, then leaped into a thick growth of scrub pines. This slowed Gray Boy down. He had to pick his way through the tangled branches and low-hanging boughs. His concentration broke and he was about to give up the chase when the deer turned again for one final maneuver. She circled up the slope to a point just above Gray Boy and then charged back downhill past his hind end, blowing one last snort through her nostrils as she went by.

The brush in the darkness was more than Gray Boy could handle. He lacked the composure of an experienced predator. He ran haphazardly after the doe, crashing and stumbling amid the pointed twigs and scraping branches. Then suddenly everything stopped with a dull thud and a flash of stars. Gray Boy had run head-on into a broad pine trunk.

The doe went off to meet her fawns. Gray Boy watched her go, then plopped his throbbing head down onto his forepaws. He momentarily passed out.

Within an hour Gray Boy had forgotten all about the deer and his swollen head. He followed another game trail to the crest of the hardwood ridge where the trail joined an old quarry road. Gray Boy's eyes shone bright in the moonlight as he paused to look back through the trees at the farm valley below. For a moment he heard what sounded like Ian calling to him. The calls were only those of the owl hooting again at the foot of the hill, but even if they had been Ian's, Gray Boy would not have gone home this time. He turned his back on the valley and headed down the dark quarry road.

6

Days went by, then weeks, and Gray Boy did not go home. The hills bristled in the chill of wintry winds. The smell of snow was in the air. Sheets of ice formed over woodland ponds. The cold didn't bother Gray Boy. His double coat of gray hair was wind- and waterproof. He raced down a rocky slope and dived into the unfrozen center of a deep quarry pool.

The water shimmered with reflections of stone walls that stood in crumbling towers around the pool. Gray Boy swam through the reflections. White clouds of breath formed in the air around his face and icicles hung from his furry chin when he climbed out of the water onto the slippery bank. He gave one tremendous shake and shed the cold water so thoroughly that he looked dry. Then he plopped onto some sunlit gravel, rested his chin on his front paws, and let out a long contented moan.

Gray Boy had chosen the abandoned quarry as his territory. Its granite walls were pock-marked with caves and crevices. There were mice, wild birds, and snowshoe rabbits to hunt. The largest of animals could live here. The sun angled down through the stone towers and warmed Gray Boy's back and ears. His baggy eyes were closed in shallow sleep, when another animal appeared on the slope near the quarry pool.

It was a female black bear. Her coarse, pitch-black coat covered a heavy layer of fat. She had come to the quarry in search of a den. When the bear caught wind of Gray Boy, she reared up on her hind legs and clawed the air. Her bellow resounded within the stone walls and Gray Boy rolled over, startled by the noise. He backed against a huge boulder. The bear came toward him. Danger was inescapable.

The big dog tucked his chin into his broad chest and charged full force into the standing bear, knocking her comically into the pool. The move gave Gray Boy a cocky confidence and, instead of running away, he wheeled around and braced on all fours to face her again.

The bear wasted no time in getting the upper hand. She plowed forward, snarling, and delivered a roundhouse blow that caught Gray Boy on the side of his throat. He tumbled backward, growling a rasping, wounded growl as the bear straddled him, clawing him each time he let his guard down. Gray Boy twisted to crawl away from her shower of blows, and as he did, the angry bear dug her teeth into his shoulder. Gray Boy reeled with pain and scrambled, squealing, out of the bear's reach.

The she-bear saw no need to continue a fight she had already won. She stood, swaying in victory, as the loser clambered over a bluff and disappeared. Gray Boy had lost his territory. Life in the wild had dealt him a sinister hand. He ran until he was far away from the bear. Then he lay down beside a smooth maple trunk and licked his wounds. Snow began sifting through the tree-tops. Gray Boy rested, whimpering in pain. More snow fell, covering him in whiteness.

7

Ian worked every weekend, splitting and stacking firewood for Randolph Agosto, in order to repay the cost of the rabbits Gray Boy had killed. It was the week before Christmas and one day after the year's first snowstorm when Mr. Agosto finally told Ian that he considered the debt cleared.

Lucy Emerson was shoveling snow out of her driveway when Ian came home with the news. She was both delighted and relieved.

When her son volunteered to shovel the rest of the drive for her, she happily handed him the shovel and went inside.

Ian liked shoveling snow. He pushed the wide shovel down the driveway and dumped the collected snow in a heap near the road. He pulled the shovel back up the drive in the path he had just cleared and turned around to begin another run.

A yellow dot popped over a knoll on the white field across the road. It was Uncle Bill, coming on his snowmobile. Ian watched as his uncle steered the sled over the snowbank and slid to a halt in the drive. The engine idled. As Uncle Bill was unsnapping his helmet, Ian told him the news about repaying Mr. Agosto. Uncle Bill smiled and gave Ian the thumbs-up sign.

"My news isn't so good," Uncle Bill said

loudly. "Lost my two beagles, rabbit huntin' up near Pine Mountain yesterday!"

Ian dropped the shovel in the snow and went to sit on the snowmobile with his uncle.

"Do you think they'll find their way home?" Ian asked.

"They may," Uncle Bill said. "But with the snow drifted deep like it is up there right now and them having such short legs, they may not be able to. I'm worried about them. I'm gonna see if I can ride up there to find them. You want to come along?"

Ian jumped at the chance. He hopped off the seat and ran to tell his mother. As he dashed up the porch steps his uncle added, "I'm not sure how far we'll get. . . . The snow's soft and there's no trail broken up that way yet. Tell your mom we'll turn around if it gets too deep."

Inside, Lucy Emerson fed a log into the wood stove. Ian stomped snowily into the house.

"Mom! Uncle Bill's outside!" He spoke hurriedly. "He says he lost Smokey and Hardtack up near Pine Mountain. He asked me to ride along on the snowmobile to help him find them."

Lucy walked to the window. She waved to her brother sitting on the shiny yellow machine. Then she turned to Ian, who was already wrapping an extra scarf around his neck and face.

"Don't worry, Mom," he said, his voice muffled by the wooly mask. "I'm dressed real warm . . . and Uncle Bill says we'll turn around if it gets too deep." Then Ian said, "Who knows? Maybe we'll find Gray Boy too!"

A look of concern flickered across Lucy Emerson's face. "Ian," she said, "we haven't seen Gray Boy in over a month. We've looked all over the valley for him. I suspect he's gone for good. If he's alive, he doesn't want to come back home." She pulled her son to her and looked him square in the eyes. "What if you do find Gray Boy in those hills? What would you do?" she asked.

Ian said all the things that had gone through his mind ever since the day Gray Boy had left for good. "I figure maybe he's got all that wildness out of his system by now. I thought I could bring him back home."

"If you got him back home . . . what then?" she asked further.

"I'll build him a wire run," Ian answered. "And a doghouse this time. Maybe I could take him fishing on a long leash. . . . Maybe he wouldn't feel like roaming off if I . . ." He stopped. His mother held him to her and kissed his forehead.

"All right, son," she said. "But if you find
Gray Boy now, he could be so wild, he won't
recognize you." She straightened Ian's hat and
fastened his coat collar under the scarves. Then
she walked him to the door.

"Be careful," she said softly. "If you see
Gray Boy, don't try to force him to go with you.
Let him come back with you on his own."

Lucy picked a pair of dry mittens from the
warming shelf over the wood stove and pulled
them onto Ian's hands. Then she gave him another kiss, and out the door he went. Ian's hopes
were high as he climbed aboard the seat behind
his uncle. They rode off in a soft whirr of engine
and snow.

The snow on the trail was deep. Ian leaned
into each turn with his uncle and ducked under
snow-laden evergreen boughs. All along the way

he tried to keep a lookout for any sign of the dogs, but the going was rough and, when they reached a steep incline in the trail, the snowmobile whined and choked.

A startled grouse thundered out of its snow hole in the trail bank and rapped clumsily against Uncle Bill's plastic windshield. Ian watched the bird sail down a slope away from them.

"Do you think we can make it all the way up Pine Mountain?" Ian asked, shouting over the engine noise.

But his uncle didn't hear him and leaned forward on the sled's seat. Ian leaned forward with him. The way had become very steep, and powdery snow whooshed by as the snowmobile climbed higher. Suddenly Ian smelled burning rubber and he could feel the machine slowing in its track. In the next instant they had bogged to a halt.

Uncle Bill sat straight up on the seat and punched the steering console. "Doggone it! That's that!" he grumbled. Then he turned around and said, "Can't do it, Ian, it's just too deep and soft. I don't want to snap that rubber drive belt way up here." He stepped off the machine into the deep snow and took hold of a front ski to pull it around in the trail. Ian helped. They yanked the heavy sled around in its track and faced it back toward home. High above, a pair of ravens flapped through the air between the treetops. "Kruuk-Kruuk," they croaked.

It was dark when the yellow snowmobile, its headlight beaming, returned to the fields in front of Ian's house. The porch light was on and inside the front window Christmas tree bulbs flickered. Lucy had hung the lights on the tree while Ian and Uncle Bill were away.

The colorful glow in the window reminded Ian that this would be the third Christmas without his dad. The festive lights also made him anticipate Christmas Day.

The snowmobile pulled into the Emerson drive and Ian jumped off. "Merry Christmas!" he wished Uncle Bill as the sled whirred around and out of the driveway. "Merry Christmas!" Uncle Bill hollered back.

8

Christmas Day was a windless white on white. Even the shadows were a kind of white.

"Kruuk . . . Kruuk." Two black dots appeared in the sky, offering contrast to the snowy scene.

"Kruuk . . . Kruuk."

The call of the ravens repeated itself on the walls of the quarry where the she-bear was now asleep. The ravens passed over the quarry and flapped on until they were directly above a small, isolated lump of land. They circled, vulture-like, then landed noisily on the carcass of a deer.

It was a first-year buck, wounded by a hunter's bullet in late autumn. The bleeding deer had run, escaping the hunter, and had finally fallen dead on a treeless crest of a lesser ridge of Pine Mountain. Now, its frozen body lay half buried under snow. The pair of ravens fought briefly for positioning on the small brown island, then settled down for a winter's feast.

Gray Boy plowed hock deep through the snow. He had been on a futile chase after a white hare when the smell of raven mixed with deer took his attention. He came upon the feeding ravens with a "Whoof!," and soon was standing alone over the carcass.

Gray Boy had gorged himself with deer meat when the two beagles appeared, seemingly out of nowhere. Smokey and Hardtack were a sad-looking pair, worn sick from wandering in the deep snow. They were hungry. The two small dogs approached the deer remains cautiously, keeping a close watch on the giant dog with every step they took.

Gray Boy rolled on his side and sank comfortably into the snow. His belly was full and the sun warmed the muscles under his dense coat. Gray Boy's shoulder wound from the bear's bite was healing over in scar tissue. The big dog saw the little dogs and, lying still, watched as they tore into what was left of the buck.

Smokey was the bigger of the two beagles. He was hunter's colors, white all over and saddled on the back and ears with black-and-brown patches. Hardtack was a stumpier beagle and completely brown except for white slippers on each of her feet and a small white spot between her eyes.

The eating restored their beagle spirit and soon the two were rollicking in the snow near Gray Boy. Their happy yaps excited him and he snapped up to a sitting position. Hardtack barked at Gray Boy, daring him to join the fun. Smokey chimed in with a hearty howl.

In the next instant Gray Boy was in the game. All three dogs sprinted in playful circles on the knoll. Gray Boy had been lonely. The amiable little beagles were as restoring to his dog mind as the deer meat had been to his belly.

That night the trio bedded down in an old cellar hole, one of the ancient landmarks in the diverse history of the Pine Mountain area. Here, a farm had prospered long ago. The cellar had thick granite boulder walls upon which a roomy house once rested. Gray Boy gently nudged his muzzle between the beagles. Then, in the silence found only in remote places, they fell asleep.

The next morning the three dogs played in simple pleasure. One dog would run away and the other two would chase it. In and out between snow-laden evergreens they raced. Each chase ended in a mock fight. The game continued into the clear, bright afternoon until each dog had a chance to chase and be chased. Eventually the dogs lay panting on the snow, played out.

Hunger pangs reached all three at the same time and their mutual discomfort created tension among them. Gray Boy's tolerance of the small dogs wore thin and he showed it with a sullen growl each time he was disturbed. Smokey took offense to the change in the big dog's attitude and barked monotonously. Whenever Smokey came a bit too close, Gray Boy snapped at the bothersome beagle.

Meanwhile, among the many trails they had created in the snow, Hardtack located the three dogs' trail from the day before. Her tail was rigid as she sniffed her way through the corridor. She followed it in and out between the trees, backtracking all the way to the treeless knoll and the remains of the buck.

There was some meat left on the deer. Hardtack chewed off a small piece and wolfed it down. Then she pulled a long strip of muscle from the deer's shoulder.

Gray Boy and Smokey were still exchanging snarls when Hardtack returned. The strip of deer meat hung from her mouth. Smokey charged down to greet his partner. Hardtack dropped the meat on the snow and together the beagles began to eat it.

Gray Boy followed slowly in Smokey's tracks and, as soon as he smelled the food, he hastened to take control.

He lunged between the beagles and

clamped his jaws over the deer meat. He maintained his stance, growling in a low rumble and shooting warning glances to the two small dogs.

Smokey backed off and cowered at Gray Boy's display, but Hardtack wouldn't. She stood her ground and growled back at Gray Boy.

Gray Boy was locked onto the food and Hardtack was crouched tensely just two feet away. Smokey hung on the perimeter of what was about to happen.

In a flash, Hardtack broke for the deer meat and bit into it.

Gray Boy unleashed a tremendous roar and pounced on the little dog. In one great motion he grasped Hardtack by the back of her neck and hurled her across the snow. Then he lowered his muzzle to the strip of meat and began eating.

The sight unnerved Smokey and he turned in fear and ran away. Hardtack, wounded but not severely, quickly followed. They ran, until by chance they came upon a wide track in the snow. It was the snowmobile trail Bill Willum and Ian had made just a week earlier. The snowmobile's tread had packed down the snow and the weary dogs walked on it easily. The rippled path led the beagles down off the mountain all the way to the warmth and care of home.

9

Bill Willum was glad to have his beagles back.
Though he was used to living alone, he missed
their company. Lately, his house had seemed
empty without them. He scooped some kibble
out of the twenty-five-pound bag and split the
amount evenly between two dog bowls. On one
bowl was lettered *Smokey;* the other read *Hardtack.* He had no idea of what had happened to
them while they had been lost, but it was obvious

that both dogs were shaken up. Hardtack's back and neck looked sore. She gingerly lowered her head to eat from her bowl. Smokey ate so hurriedly that he choked on his food a few times before he was finished.

There was a short familiar knock. The door pushed open and Lucy and Ian entered, letting in with them a rush of frigid outside air. Lucy Emerson was carrying a steaming, covered dish. She had brought supper. Bill smelled hot stew. "For me?" he asked in a comically grateful tone.

"No, Bill, I brought this for those two pups of yours!" Lucy joked back.

Ian laughed. Uncle Bill laughed with him.

Ian went over to Smokey and Hardtack. He stooped and gently patted both their heads. He felt Hardtack trembling.

"What do you think happened to Hardtack

up on that mountain, Uncle Bill?" Ian asked.

"I can't tell," said Uncle Bill, "something got her by the back of the neck, though. See—she's sore, and there's some dried blood on her hair."

Ian looked at the dried blood and imagined a big ugly bear attacking the little dog. "Probably was a bear," Ian said.

But his uncle said, "No, bears are all denned up now. I think it must have been a coyote or maybe even a wild dog."

Ian, Uncle Bill, and Lucy all thought of Gray Boy. Then Uncle Bill said, "No, as a matter of fact, I'm sure it wasn't another dog. It had to have been either a coyote or a bobcat, maybe even a fisher."

Ian was still thinking about Gray Boy. "Do you think Gray Boy could be alive?" he asked.

Uncle Bill began to help set the table for their supper of stew. He was about to answer Ian's question when Lucy spoke out. "Ian, if Gray Boy is still alive, he's changed."

"He'd have to have been killing to eat," added Uncle Bill. Then he took Ian by the shoulder and walked him over to the picture window. It presented a spectacular view of the whole Pine Mountain area. "Look at that wilderness, boy. Do you know what it's like up there this time of year?" Bill Willum pointed to one of Pine Mountain's many forested slopes.

"The snow in those woods is over four feet deep now and it's cold enough there to freeze a body overnight!" Gently, he turned his nephew around toward him. "I don't think Gray Boy is alive, Ian. Look at the beagles. See the condition they're in from little more than a week up there.

It's time you tried to forget about ever finding Gray Boy, son."

Uncle Bill walked Ian over to the table and they sat down to eat. Lucy Emerson made them pause to say grace. Then she began dishing out the stew.

"I know!" Uncle Bill said brightly as he buttered a slice of bread. "I've been thinking of breeding Smokey and Hardtack. They're not brother and sister, you know."

"I didn't know!" said Lucy, delighted at the thought of the beagles having puppies.

"And Ian, you will have the pick of their litter!" Uncle Bill glanced at his sister for her approval. Lucy approved. Ian perked up at the notion.

"I'll build the new pup a wire kennel to stay in while I'm away at school," Ian said deci-

sively. "Maybe we can go rabbit hunting together, Uncle Bill?"

"You bet!" promised Uncle Bill.

Lucy Emerson hummed a happy tune as she
took another helping of stew.

10

Winter finally was coming to an end. The hours of daylight increased. Slowly, snow began to melt. The thaw encouraged more open activity among Pine Mountain's wild animals. Gray Boy hunted mice and birds and kept himself alive. But the increasingly frequent scent of deer roaming out of their winter yards gnawed at him.

One day, while Gray Boy was on the track of a deer, an even more urgent scent captured his interest. It led him to a small hollow and a frozen beaver pond. The pond was in the final stages of melting before breakup. In its center, the beavers' lodge of sticks stuck up through the ice and snow.

At one place near the edge of the frozen pond, there was a small hole through the ice, which the beavers had recently made. They had been venturing out over land to cut nearby saplings for fresh food. All around their plunge hole the scent of beaver was strong. It was primarily this scent wafting through the air that had lured Gray Boy to the hollow.

Gray Boy spotted something dark moving near the plunge hole. It was a fisher. The fisher, also attracted to the place by the scent of beaver, had been investigating around the rim of the hole when it had slipped down into the black oval and had become caught in a beaver trap that had been set in the shallow water. The fisher's right foreleg was clamped in the jaws of the trap, which was chained to a length of maple buried in the heavy, wet snow up on the pond bank. The large, sleek weasel was angry and frightened. It tugged at the uncompromising steel.

Gray Boy stood on the edge of small timber and studied this strange animal. Winter had been harsh in the Pine Mountain area and, aside from the animals he hunted and the two beagles, Gray Boy had been alone.

Gray Boy lifted his nose to the scent of the trapped animal. It was an odd, perplexing odor. The musky smell of the frightened fisher recalled that of the marauding skunk in the Emersons' trash. The fisher had tugged at its trapped leg until the delicate fur hung loosely around raw skin. It arched its powerful back another time and pulled, trying to budge the maple stake that held the chain. But the stake didn't move. In its pain and struggling, the fisher hadn't noticed Gray Boy's slow approach.

The dog wanted a closer look. He stopped about twenty feet from the fisher. Gray Boy's eyes barely blinked as he watched.

The fisher was about three feet long, half of which was tail. Its body was lean and muscular. It had five toes on each foot and each toe had a long sharp claw.

The fisher suddenly spun around and faced Gray Boy. Its catlike hiss bristled the hairs down the dog's back, causing Gray Boy to veer backward. Then the fisher lunged forward with a growling snarl, slapping links of chain against the ice.

The fisher lunged again and this time Gray Boy saw the trap around the weasel's bloody right leg. He smelled the blood and metal and musk and he jumped forward barking and growling.

The fisher whirled around, snapping its jaws in warning. Gray Boy ran a wide circle around the tormented animal. Then, in a low crouching advance, he closed the distance between them. The fisher became silent, coiled and ready to spring with all the ferocity of its tribe. Gray Boy drew close and the weasel bared its fangs and snarled a low foreboding snarl.

The sight of such coiled fury shook Gray Boy's confidence. He charged haphazardly, counteracting his impulse to retreat. The fisher's fangs ripped into Gray Boy's stomach. And again, this time tearing into his groin! Gray Boy yelped and shrieked. The weasel's speed was overwhelming. Its sharp claws raked across Gray Boy's ribs. In attempting to escape fang and claw,

Gray Boy slipped into the ice hole and got his hind leg tangled in the trap's chain. As he struggled to free himself, the fisher lashed into him again.

At last Gray Boy broke away and raced up the sloping pond bank into the birches. He had not delivered even one blow in the encounter. The fisher snapped and hissed as the dog put space between them, leaving a trail of blood on the ground. Gray Boy's wounds were deep, draining strength from his body. He felt no need greater than that of lying down.

A warm puddle of blood formed on the snow where he lay. The blood puddle filled until a trickle of it flowed down the wooded slope—a dark, red line on a surface of white.

11

The countryside rolled by the school-bus window as Ian rode home. He could see the snowy form of Pine Mountain. As usual, the image of Gray Boy formed in his mind, but he pushed it away and thought about Hardtack. Now she was expecting pups and one of them—the pick of the litter—was going to be his. As the school bus neared the village, the last stop before Ian's, he remembered that he needed to stop at the village store for a pack of loose-leaf paper and some other school supplies.

Ian reached in his coat pocket for his list as the bus driver pulled up to the corner and swung the doors open.

Emma White was at the counter with a customer when Ian walked into the store.

"Hi, Ian!" she greeted him as she was ringing up a counterful of items.

Ian waved and smiled. He walked down an aisle to the back of the store where Emma kept the stationery. He could hear the customer talking to Mrs. White up front.

"Sure turned out to be a nice day," the man offered cordially. Emma nodded to him. Then he added, "I had a fright this morning though!"

It was obvious that the man was bursting to tell a story, so Emma leaned back on the register and gave him her attention. Ian listened too.

The customer began. "I was tendin' a beaver trap up on Pine Mountain . . . there," he pointed out the store window to a spot in the hills, "when I came across this wounded dog lying on the snow."

"A dog?" Emma said, and glanced down the aisle at Ian.

"Yeah, a dog," the trapper repeated. "A huge, gray dog."

Ian raced up the aisle. He startled the man with his question. "Like a Newfoundland?"

"I think it was!" the man said. "And it was hurt real bad. Had lost a lot of blood from a gash in its gut. I figured it must have run into the fisher that had accidentally gotten caught in my trap."

Ian went pale. "Did you bring him down? Is the dog with you? Where'd you . . ."

The trapper broke into Ian's line of questions saying loudly, "Bring him down? Boy, I'm lucky he didn't bring *me* down! That animal nearly ripped my throat open!"

Ian's hopes collapsed and the man saw the disappointment in his face. He offered an apology. "Hey, that your dog, pal? I'm sorry. I tried to help, but it jumped me. It's hurt bad."

Ian looked up at the trapper and asked, "Where on the mountain did you say you saw him?"

"The closest ridge, on a timbered slope near a beaver pond. You could follow my snowshoe trail from the town road right up to the spot," the trapper said.

Ian slapped his money on the counter and left with only a few of the things he needed. He didn't wait for change. The trapper rushed to the door and called after him, "Be careful, that dog may have been tame once, but he's a vicious animal now!"

Lucy Emerson had spent her afternoon attacking some household repairs that, all winter, she had put off doing. She had just finished replacing a washer in a leaky faucet, and was cleaning up the sink, when she heard the scraping of Ian's steps running on the porch.

"Mom . . . Mom!" he called anxiously as he entered.

"What is it, Ian? Are you all right?"

Ian plopped the bag from the store on the table and reached over the door for his father's deer rifle. "What in the world do you think you are going to do with that gun?" his mother asked.

Ian checked the rifle's chamber to be sure it was clear, the way his dad had taught him to.

Then he said, "Some trapper found Gray Boy on the mountain this morning! He's hurt bad. . . ."

"The trapper?" Lucy asked.

"No, Gray Boy. This guy came across him near a beaver pond this side of Pine Mountain. He said a huge, gray dog was lying hurt. He had a deep gash in his gut and was losing lots of blood!"

Lucy was alarmed. Ian could see that she was about to lay down the law and forbid him to go after his dog. Before she could say anything, he explained, "Gray Boy attacked this man, Mom. I never thought he'd attack a person. Anyway, he must be delirious with pain. I can't stand thinking of him lying up there!" Ian buckled on his father's cartridge belt, wearing it over his shoulder rather than around his small waist.

His mother protested. "That dog's been in the wilderness for months! What if he attacks you?"

"That's why I need the .30-30," Ian answered. "But if he does know me, maybe I can help. Maybe I can get him home. I'll take the toboggan to haul him down."

Lucy took the rifle from her son's hands and laid it on the kitchen table. "No. . . . You're not going up there. That's it!" she commanded. Then she walked out of the room.

Ian quietly lifted the rifle from the table and pushed five .30-caliber cartridges into its magazine. Then he left.

Lucy Emerson was frantic as she explained the situation on the phone to her brother Bill.

"It's only a couple of hours before it will get dark, Bill. Ian may get up the mountain all right, but it will be too dark for him to get back. He may get lost. Bill, the dog is dangerous. . . . He may hurt Ian!"

Bill Willum said he'd leave right away and bring Ian home. "Don't worry, Lucy," he said. "The snow's settled and firm now. I can easily ride the snowmobile up to Ian. I'll just follow his tracks to find him."

They both hung up. Lucy walked to the window and saw her son's trail. It crossed the white cornfield and faded in the distance in the direction of the mountain.

12

Ian followed the trapper's trail in the snow. By the time he reached the beaver pond, the sun was going down. Mist was rising off the melting ice. All Ian could see were the faint lines of birch and ironwood covering the sloping land around the hollow. Ian took his snowshoes off, stood them up in the snow, and stepped onto the slippery ice of the pond. He studied the pond's circumference. A red smear on the opposite bank caught his eye and he headed toward it, pulling the toboggan behind him.

The signs were clear. Ian could see the trapper's story rewritten in the snow. There was the impression where the huge dog had been lying, the blood from its wound, trailing down the slope, and the prone imprint of the trapper where the dog had knocked him down. Ian thought that perhaps he was looking for a mad dog after all! He levered a cartridge into the rifle's chamber.

Gray Boy's tracks had gone off uphill away from the trapper's imprint, but Ian could see, even in the fading light, that the dog's bloody trail turned and veered back down to the fringes of the tiny pond.

As Ian walked on the pond ice again, he heard a faint whimpering coming from behind some nearby alders. He saw Gray Boy behind the brushy trees, lying on the snow. Ian abandoned the toboggan and with the rifle ready in his hands, he stepped closer, stopping on a gray patch of ice.

Gray Boy lifted his head and stared through the curtain of alders at the figure with the gun. He growled a low growl. Ian lifted the rifle, thumbed back the hammer, and rested his finger gently on the trigger. If he had to shoot his own dog, he was going to do it quickly. Just then he felt himself sink an inch or so in his tracks. The ice under him gave way and, in the next instant, he dropped down into the ice-cold water.

Ian floundered in the black hole. His woolen clothing became waterlogged and heavy. The more he struggled, the deeper he sank. The stinging water numbed his hands and face. He was losing strength. He lunged upward, momentarily getting his head out in the air, and yelled desperately as he began going back under.

"GRAY BOY!"

Gray Boy had not heard his name in months. An image of the past flashed through his mind—he and Ian at the fishing hole. Something clicked inside him. Gray Boy rose to his feet and saw Ian struggling in the water. Drawing on the strength left in him, the big dog hobbled painfully over the frozen surface of the pond and plunged into the icy hole.

Underwater, Gray Boy clamped his soft mouth on Ian's wool coat collar. Then, with a watery grunt, he swam to the surface. He pulled the boy to the ice rim and heaved himself and Ian out of the water.

When Ian had caught his breath, he crawled over the ice to where Gray Boy lay in a circle of blood-stained water. The shivering boy could see the dog's huge rib cage heaving hollow tremulous breaths. Weeping, Ian leaned gently over the great dog's body and laid his reddened face on Gray Boy's wet fur. He spoke a soft "Thank you," and kept his head on Gray Boy's chest, listening to heartbeats and breathing, until both stopped. Gray Boy was dead.

With a cold-numbed hand, Ian lovingly stroked his dog's massive forehead. He whispered, "Good boy . . . good boy."

In the distance, the sound of Uncle Bill's snowmobile whined steadily as it drew ever closer to the darkening hollow.

Jim Arnosky wrote *Gray Boy* over a ten-year period, following a sad and frustrating experience with a large gray dog he owned. He drew on this, and more enjoyable experiences he's had with other dogs, to tell this story of a dog neither wild nor tame.

Arnosky is well known as an author, artist, and naturalist, and has written many highly successful books for young readers. His *Drawing from Nature,* an ALA Notable Book, was called "a bible on the art of awareness" by Eric Sloane. The book and its companion, *Drawing Life in Motion,* were described as "luminous tributes to Arnosky's powers of observation" in *Science 84*.

In constant touch with the natural world, Jim Arnosky is able to share his experiences with readers of all ages. In its starred review of *Raccoons and Ripe Corn,* a picture book for very young children, *School Library Journal* declared, "The book is so simple—yet it has long-range, satisfying, repeated appeal for the youngest patrons."

Jim Arnosky and his family live in a two-hundred-year-old farmhouse in rural Vermont.